# A New True Book

# SPACE

## By Illa Podendorf

*This "true book" was prepared
under the direction of
Illa Podendorf,
formerly with the Laboratory School,
University of Chicago*

CHILDRENS PRESS, CHICAGO

Astronaut Anna Fishers wears a life-support suit designed for work outside the space shuttle.

PHOTO CREDITS

National Aeronautics and Space Administration (NASA)—Cover, 2, 9, 10, 14, 20, 30, 34 (2 photos), 35, 37 (2 photos), 38, 40, 41, 45

Rockwell International—42 (© Charles Harbutt, Archive Pictures, Inc.), 43

Lynn M. Stone—4

Tony Freeman—6

Jerry Hennen—23

National Museum of History and Technology, Smithsonian Institution—16

National Air and Space Museum, Smithsonian Institution—17, 18, 33

RCA—28

Hughes Aircraft Company—32

John Forsberg—12, 13, 19, 25, 27

COVER—Painting of future space shuttles working on the construction of an orbiting platform. The structure at right is designed to capture an earth-approaching asteroid.

Library of Congress Cataloging in Publication Data

Podendorf, Illa.
    Space.

    (A New true book)
    Rev. ed. of: The true book of space. © 1959.
    Includes index.
    Summary: Defines in simple terms the characteristics of outer space, satellites, and the principles of flight through space.
    1. Space sciences—Juvenile literature.
2. Space flight—Juvenile literature.
3. Outer space—Juvenile literature. [1. Space sciences. 2. Space flight. 3. Outer space]
I. Title.
QB500.22.P6  1982      500.5      82-4507
ISBN 0-516-01650-4          AACR2

# TABLE OF CONTENTS

Where Is Space?... **5**

What Is Outer Space?... **8**

How Do We Travel in Space with Air in It?... **15**

How Do We Travel in Outer Space?... **21**

What Is a Satellite?... **26**

People Can Travel in Outer Space... **33**

Words You Should Know... **46**

Index... **47**

**4**

# WHERE IS SPACE?

When we look into the sky, we look into space.

The sky is the biggest space that we know anything about.

All of the spaces around us have air in them.

There is air in every crack and hole on this earth. There is air in the ground and in the water.

When we look into the sky, we look into air. We cannot see air. Air has no color.

We can feel air when the wind blows. Wind is moving air.

There is air inside of us, too. When we take a deep breath, we take air into the little spaces in our lungs.

We cannot live without air.

# WHAT IS
# OUTER SPACE?

Outer space stretches out in all directions beyond the earth.

This space probably has very little in it. Scientists think that it has no air of the kind we know in it.

This satellite, called Landsat, was designed to study the earth's natural resources. Huge sections of land can be seen from a satellite in orbit around the earth.

This faraway space is so big that a trip into it would last longer than we can imagine, if we traveled at the speeds we know on earth.

The Voyager spacecraft took photographs of Saturn
and its rings. From them an artist
drew this picture of the Saturn system.

No one knows how far
away outer space goes.
We can see some things
in outer space. We can
see the moon, sun, planets,
and faraway stars.

We can see a meteor when it comes into the earth's air. A meteor is a piece of a kind of rock from outer space. It burns up from heat made by rubbing against bits of air. We call it a "shooting star."

The moon is closer to
the earth than the sun or
any of the planets.

Some of the planets are
closer to the earth than
the sun is.

Some planets are farther
from the earth than the
sun is.

The stars are much
farther away than the
moon, the sun, and the
planets.

Earth as seen from outer space.

Outer space seems to have no end to it. The space close to the earth that has air in it is much smaller than the faraway outer space.

# HOW DO WE TRAVEL IN SPACE WITH AIR IN IT?

There are many ways to travel in space that has air in it.

Scientists keep finding better ways for us to travel.

They invented the steam engine and people began to travel in boats and trains.

Model T. Ford 1913

A few years later, scientists invented the gasoline engine.

Some engines can burn other fuels besides gasoline. Some engines burn oil.

But all of these engines must have oxygen from the air to help the fuels burn.

The gasoline engine made it possible for airplanes to have power enough to fly. Scientists worked to build better engines and faster airplanes.

*Spirit of St. Louis* In 1927 Charles Lindbergh became the first man to fly alone across the Atlantic Ocean without stopping.

In 1947 the Bell X-1, named *Glamorous Glennis,* was the first piloted jet to travel faster than the speed of sound.

Jet planes do not work in the same way that planes with gasoline engines and propellers work. But they, too, must have oxygen to burn their fuels.

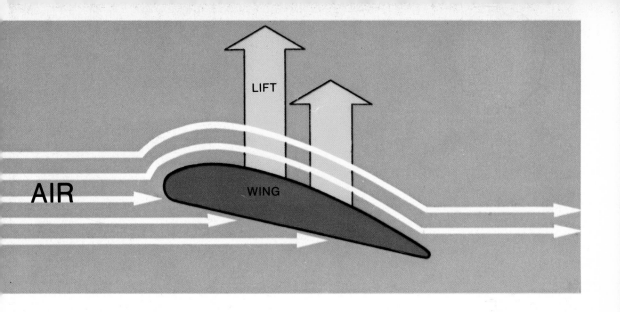

All planes need air to
give oxygen to the motors.

They also need air
flowing over the wings to
hold them up.

The air that we travel
through in trains, cars,
boats, and planes is close
to the earth.

The space shuttle, *Columbia,* lifts off on its second space mission.

# HOW DO WE TRAVEL IN OUTER SPACE?

As you know, scientists have found some ways to travel in outer space— space that does not have air in it.

A rocket that can go into outer space has been invented. A rocket carries its own oxygen and fuel with it.

Rockets can travel several miles in one second. This is much faster than a jet plane can go.

But when a rocket ship runs out of fuel or oxygen in outer space, there is no way to get more.

The first stage of the Saturn V rocket.

Scientists have made one, two, three, and four stage rockets. Each stage carries the oxygen or fuel it needs.

One of the rockets starts the ship into space. When it runs out of fuel, it falls away.

The second rocket takes over and sends the ship farther.

After the second rocket falls away, the third one sends the ship still farther, and so on.

Once the ship is beyond the air of the earth, it can keep going without any fuel.

There is no air to push
against it and to slow
down its speed. It may
move into an orbit and
circle the earth. It may
become a satellite.

# WHAT IS A SATELLITE?

A satellite is a follower. It follows something bigger and greater than it is.

The earth has a satellite. It is called the moon.

The moon follows the earth as the earth travels around the sun.

The moon moves around the earth in a path called an orbit. The moon stays in its orbit because the pull of the earth keeps it there.

RCA communications satellite, Satcom, in earth orbit.

Rockets have sent man-made satellites into space. These satellites go around the earth in orbits of their own. The paths of the man-made satellites are between the earth and the orbit of the moon.

Instruments in satellites have sent messages back to earth. From these messages scientists have learned many things about outer space.

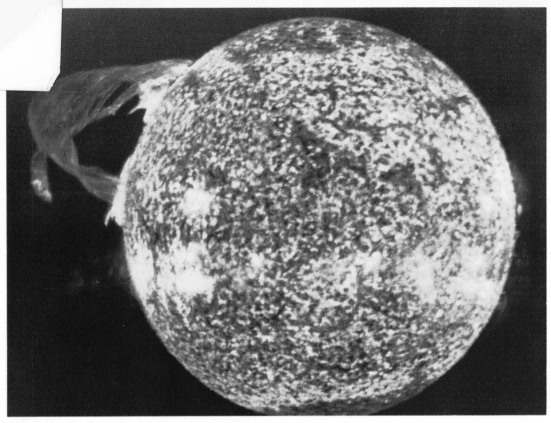

Skylab, a manned spacecraft, took this photograph of the sun
during a spectacular solar flare (at left). All the planets
in our solar system orbit around the sun.

Scientists have learned
that the sun's rays make
things very hot in some
parts of outer space.

Scientists have found out that things can be very cold in some parts of outer space.

They have learned that it is very dark in outer space.

They have learned that the sun's rays can be dangerous in outer space.

International communications satellites, called Intelsat, are bigger than ever. The newest and biggest satellite is on the left; the oldest and smallest one is on the far right.

They have learned that outer space is silent—a place without a sound.

What scientists have learned has helped them plan safe ways for people to make trips in outer space.

# PEOPLE CAN TRAVEL IN OUTER SPACE

Many questions had to be answered before scientists could send animals and, later, men into space.

*The Space Mural—A Cosmic View* by Robert McCall is on display at the National Air and Space Museum in Washington, D.C.

Guion S. Bluford, Jr., a lieutenant colonel in the Air Force, (left) and Dr. Sally K. Ride (right) are space shuttle crewmembers scheduled for future space missions

Now astronauts have journeyed into space. On each trip they learn many things.

The people at the mission control center at the Johnson Space Center oversee all of the activities on a spacecraft during its mission. The huge map in the front of the room shows the path the spacecraft is taking as it orbits the earth.

Scientists have found ways to keep people safe during the take off of the rocket ship and during the return to earth.

The space shuttle has been built to travel in and out of space again and again. The space shuttle could be used to carry people, equipment, and supplies to space stations.

Above: View of the space shuttle returning to earth.
Below: An artist's drawing, based on scientific studies, shows
a future space station.

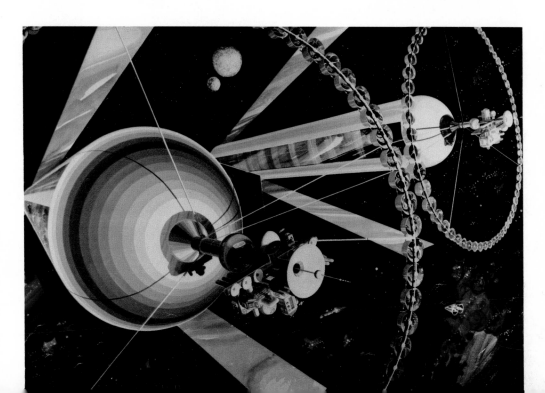

The space shuttle will be used to build space colonies.

Every day scientists learn more about outer space. They have found answers to many problems. But they are working on many more of them.

A space station or platform may someday be built out in space.

In the year 2100 people living in space may build places that look like this mountain valley. These scenes will be made from materials taken from the moon and asteroids. Energy would come from the sun and the entire colony would be enclosed. Remember there is no oxygen in space.

Space ships or rockets may get more fuel at the space station.

Space ships might be built or put together at the space station.

Part of a space colony would be used to grow food.
This drawing shows what a space farm might look like.
On some levels there might be food crops, such as wheat,
other areas would be used to raise cattle and fish.

Scientists are working on new ways of supplying the food, water, and air that would be needed on long trips into outer space.

The time may come
when much more will be
known about traveling at
great speed and building
better rockets.

Scientists may find new
fuels for space travel. They
are trying to find a way to
use atomic energy in
space ships. Someday
scientists may use power
from the sun for space
travel.

Close-ups of
the Challenger
spacecraft
being built.

Some scientists think that all of the problems of long space trips can never be overcome.

Other scientists believe that the most important problems will be solved in a few years, and that men and women can make long trips safely in outer space.

*One Man's Lifetime*
by Roland O. Powell.
This painting
shows how methods
of transportation
have changed in
the last 150 years.
Pictured are the
Wright brothers'
plane, the Corsair
jet, a Lunar Roving
Vehicle, Skylab
Space Station,
the American Apollo
and the Soviet
Soyuz spacecraft,
and the space
shuttle.

Someday many of us
will travel in and out of
outer space and later tell
about our trips.

# WORDS YOU SHOULD KNOW

**astronaut**(AST • roh • nawt) — a person trained to fly in a spacecraft

**atomic energy**(ah • TOM • ick EN • er • gee) — energy that comes from action of atoms. An atom is the smallest bit of an element that can exist alone.

**energy**(EN • er • gee) — power to do work

**engine**(EN • jin) — a machine using the energy of steam, gasoline, oil, or wood

**fuel**(FYOOL) — anything that is burned to give off heat or energy

**gasoline**(gas • oh • LEEN) — fuel made from petroleum or natural gas

**gravity**(GRAV • ih • tee) — the force that the earth and other heavenly bodies have that pulls other things toward their center

**meteor**(MEE • tee • or) — piece of stone or metal from outer space

**orbit**(OR • bit) — the path that something takes in space

**outer space**(OUT • er SPAYSS) — space beyond the earth's atmosphere

**oxygen**(OX • ih • jin) — colorless, odorless gas part of the earth's atmosphere. Air has oxygen in it.

**planets** — the nine outer-space bodies that move in orbits around the sun; the planets are Mercury, Venus, Earth, Mars, Jupiter, Saturn, Uranus, Neptune, and Pluto

**rocket**(ROCK • et) — a missile; an engine that uses a fast-burning fuel mixed with oxygen. This combination gives the rocket great power on take off.

**space shuttle** — a space ship that takes off from the earth by rocket power, orbits the earth, and then lands back on earth like an airplane

**space station** — a large structure that someday may be built in outer space to orbit the earth

**sun** — the closest star to our earth; it gives us heat and light

# INDEX

air, 5-7, 8, 11, 14, 17, 18, 24, 25
airplanes, 17-19, 22
astronauts, 34
atomic energy, 42
boats, 15, 19
breathing air, 7
cars, 19
cold in outer space, 31
darkness in outer space, 31
earth, 8, 11, 13, 14, 19, 24-27, 29
engines, 15-17
fuels, 16-18, 21-24, 40, 42
gasoline engine, 16, 17, 18
heat in outer space, 30
jet planes, 18, 22
man-made satellites, 29
meteors, 11
moon, 10, 13, 26, 27, 29
orbits, 25, 27, 29
outer space, travel in, 9, 21-25, 32-45
outer space, what it is, 8-14
outer space, what scientists have learned, 30-32
oxygen, 17, 18, 19, 21-23
planets, 10, 13
propellers, 18

rockets, 21-24, 29, 40, 42
rocket ships, 22, 24, 25, 35
rocket stages, 23, 24
satellites, 25-29
satellites, man-made, 29
scientists, 8, 15-17, 21, 23, 29-33, 35, 39, 41, 42, 44
"shooting stars," 11
sky, as space, 5
sound in outer space, 32
space, where it is, 5-7
space ships, 40, 42
space shuttle, 36
space stations, 36, 39, 40
space with air in it, travel in, 15-19
stars, 10, 13
steam engine, 15
sun, 10, 13, 26, 30, 31, 42
sun's rays in outer space, 30, 31
trains, 15, 19
travel in outer space, 9, 21-25, 32-45
travel in space with air in it, 15-19
wind, 7
wings, 19

*About the Author*

*Born and raised in western Iowa, Illa Podendorf has had experience teaching science at both elementary and high school levels. For many years she served as head of the Science Department, Laboratory School, University of Chicago and is currently consultant on the series of True Books and author of many of them. A pioneer in creative teaching, she has been especially successful in working with the gifted child.*